Thralls of the Endless Night

Thralls of the Endless Night

by Leigh Brackett

The Ship held an ancient secret that meant life to the dying east-aways of the void. Then Wes Kirk revealed the secret to his people's enemies—and found that his betrayal meant the death of the girl he loved.

Wes Kirk shut his teeth together, hard. He turned his back on Ma Kirk and the five younger ones huddled around the box of heat-stones and went to the doorway, padding soft and tight with the anger in him.

He shoved the curtain of little skins aside and crouched there with his thick shoulders fitted into the angle of the jamb, staring out, cold wind threading in across his splayed and naked feet.

The hackles rose golden and stiff across Kirk's back. He said carefully,

"I would like to kill the Captain and the First Officer and the Second Officer and all the little Officers, and the Engineers, and all their families."

His voice carried inside on the wind eddies. Ma Kirk yelled,

"Wes! You come here and let that curtain down! You want us all to freeze?" Her dark-furred shoulders moved rhythmically over the rocking child. She added sharply, "Besides, that's fool's talk, Jakk Randl's talk, and only gets the sucking-plant."

"Who's to hear it?" Kirk raised his heavy overlids and let his pupils widen, huge liquid drops spreading black across his eyeballs, sucking the dim grey light into themselves, forcing line and shape out of blurred nothingness. He made no move to drop the curtain.

The same landscape he had stared at since he was able to crawl by himself away from the box of heat-stones. Flat grey plain running right and left to the little curve of the horizon. Rocks on it, and edible moss. Wind-made gullies with grey shrubs thick in their bottoms, guarding their sour white berries with thorns and sacs of poisoned dust that burst when touched.

Between the fields and the gullies there were huts like his own, sunk into the earth and sodded tight. A lot of huts, but not as many as there had been, the old ones said. The Hans died, and the huts were empty, and the wind and the earth took them back again.

Kirk raised his shaggy head. The light of the yellow star they called Sun caught in the huge luminous blackness of his eyes.

Beyond the Hansquarter, just where the flat plain began to rise, were the Engineers. Not many of them any more. You could see the dusty lumps where the huts had been, the tumbled heaps of metal that might have meant something once, a longer time ago than anyone could remember. But there were still plenty of huts standing. Two hands and one hand and a thumb of them, full of Engineers who said how the furrows should be laid for the planting but did nothing about the tilling of them.

And beyond the Engineers—the Officers.

The baby cried. Ma Kirk shrilled at her son, and two of the younger ones fought over a bone with no meat on it, rolling and snapping on the dirt floor. Kirk shifted his head forward to shut out the sound of them and followed the line of the plain upward with sullen, glowing eyes.

The huts of the Engineers were larger than those in the Hansquarter. The huts of the Officers were not much larger than the Engineers', but there were more of them and they climbed higher up the grey slope. Five, nearly six hands of them, with the Captain's metal-roofed place highest of all.

Highest and nearest, right under the titanic shape lifting jagged against the icy stars from the crest of the ridge.

The Ship.

Kirk's voice was soft in his thick throat. "I would like to kill them," he said. "I would like to kill them all."

"Yah!" cried a shrill voice over his shoulder. "All but the Captain's yellow daughter!"

*

Kirk spun angrily around. Lil, next below himself, danced back out of reach, her kilt of little skins flying around her thin hips.

"Yah!" she said again, and wrinkled her flat nose. "I've seen you looking at her. All yellow from head to foot and beautiful pink lids to her eyes. You wouldn't kill *her*, I bet!"

"I bet I'll half kill you if you don't shut up!"

Lil stuck out her tongue. Kirk aimed a cuff at her. She danced behind his arm and jerked the curtain down and shot away again, making two jumps over the brawling young ones and the box of heat-stones.

She squatted demurely beside Ma Kirk and said, as though nothing had happened, "Ma says will you please not let so much heat out."

Kirk didn't say anything. He started to walk around the heat box. Lil yelled, "Ma!"

The young ones stopped fighting, scuttling out of reach and watching with bright moist eyes, grinning. The baby had reached the hiccoughing stage.

Ma Kirk said, "Sit down, or go pick on somebody your own size."

Kirk stopped. "Aw, I wasn't going to hurt her. She has to be so smart!" He leaned forward to glare at Lil. "And I would so kill the Captain's daughter!"

The baby was quiet. Ma Kirk laid it down in a nest of skins put close to the heat and said wearily:

"You men, always talking about killing! Haven't we enough trouble without that?"

Kirk looked at the little box of heat-stones, his pupils shrinking.

"Maybe there'd be less trouble for us."

Lil poked her shock of black hair around Ma Kirk's knee. Her big eyes glowed in the feeble light.

She said, "You men! He's no man, Ma. He's just a little boy who has to stay behind and shoo the beetles out of the fields."

The young ones giggled, well out of reach. Lil's thin body was strung tight, quivering to move. "Besides," she demanded, "what have the Officers and the Engineers ever done to you that you should want to kill them—all but the Captain's yellow daughter?"

Kirk's big heavy chest swelled. "Ma," he said, "you make that brat shut up or I'll whale her, anyhow."

Ma Kirk looked at him. "Your Pa's still big enough to whale you, young man! Now you stop it, both of you."

"All right," said Kirk sullenly. He squatted down, holding his hands over the heat. His back twitched with the cold, but it was nice to have his belly warm, even if it was empty. "Wish Pa'd hurry up. I'm hungry. Hope they killed meat."

Ma Kirk sighed. "Seems like meat gets scarcer all the time, like the heat-stones."

"Maybe," said Kirk heavily, "it all goes to the same place."

Lil snorted. "And where's that, Smarty?"

His anger forced out the forbidden words.

"Where everybody says, stupid! Into the Ship."

There was suddenly a lot of silence in the room. The word "Ship" hung there, awesome and accusing. Ma Kirk's eyes flicked to the curtain over the door and back to her son.

"Don't you say things like that, Wes! You don't know."

"It's what everybody says. Why else would they guard the Ship the way they do? We can't even get near the outside of it."

Lil tossed her head. "Well neither do they."

"Not when we can see 'em, no. Of course not. But how do we know they haven't got ways of getting into the Ship that don't show from the plain? Jakk says a lot goes on that we don't know about."

He got up, forcing his belief at them with his big square hands.

"There must be something in the Ship that they don't want us to have. Something valuable, something they want to keep for themselves. What else could it be but heat-stones and maybe dried meat?"

"We don't know, Wes! The Ship is—well, we shouldn't talk about it. And the Officers wouldn't do that. If they wanted us killed off they'd let the Piruts in on us, or the shags, and let 'em finish us quick. Freezing and starving would take too long. There'd be too many of us if we found out, or got mad."

Kirk snorted. "You women know so much. If they let the shags or the Piruts in on us, how could they stop 'em before they killed everybody, including the Officers? As for slow death—well, they think we're dumb. They've kept us away from the Ship ever since the *Crash*, and nobody knows how long ago that was. They think they can go on doing it. They think we'd never suspect."

"Yah!" said Lil sharply. "You just like to talk. Why should the Officers want us killed off anyhow?"

Kirk looked at the thin fuzzy baby curled tight in the skins.

"There aren't enough heat-stones to go around any more. Why should they let their young ones cry with the cold?"

*

There was silence in the room again. Kirk felt it, thick and choky. His heart kicked against his ribs. He was scared, suddenly. He'd never talked that much before. It was the baby, crying in the cold, that set him off. Suppose someone had heard him. Suppose he was reported for a mutineer. That meant the sucking-plant....

"Listen!" said Ma Kirk.

Nerves crackled icily all over Kirk's skin. But there wasn't any need to listen. The noise rolled in over them. It hit rock faces polished by the wind, and the drifts of crystalline pebbles, and it splintered into a tangle of echoes that came from everywhere at once, but there was no mistaking it. No need even to use sensitive earcups to locate its source.

The great alarm gong by the Captain's hut.

Kirk began to move, very swiftly and quietly. Before the third gong stroke hit them he had his spear and his sling and was already lifting aside the door curtain.

Ma Kirk said stiffly, "Which way are they coming?"

Kirk's ears twitched. He sorted the gong sounds, and the wind, and found a whisper underneath them, rushing up out of the gullied plain.

Kirk pointed. "From the west. Piruts, I think."

Ma Kirk sucked in her breath. Her voice had no tone in it. "Your Pa went hunting that way."

"Yeah," said Kirk. "I'll watch out for him."

He glanced back just before he let the curtain drop. The pale glow of the heat-stones picked dots of luminous blackness out of the gloom, where the still breathless faces were, watching him. He saw the blurred shapes of clay cooking pots, of low bed frames, of huddled bodies. The baby began to whimper again.

THRALLS OF THE ENDLESS NIGHT

Kirk shivered in the cold wind. "Lil," he said. "I would, too, kill the Captain's yellow daughter."

"Yah," said Lil. "Go chase the beetles away."

There was no conviction in her voice. The wind was freezing on Kirk's bare feet. He dropped the curtain and went across the plain.

Men and youths like himself, old enough to fight, were spilling out of low doorways and forming companies on the flat ground. Kirk spotted Jakk Randl and fell in beside him. They stood with their backs to the wind, stamping and shivering, their head-hair and scant fur clouts blown straight out.

Randl nudged Kirk's elbow. "Look at 'em," he said, and coughed. He was always coughing, jerking his thin sharp face back and forth. Kirk could have broken his brittle light-furred body in two. All Randl's strength was in his eyes. The pupils were always spread, always hot with some bitter force, always probing. He wasn't much older than Kirk.

Kirk looked up the hill. Officers were running from the huts below the gaunt, dead Ship. They didn't look so different from the Hans, only they were built a little taller and lighter, less bowed and bunchy in the shoulders, quicker on their feet.

Kirk stepped behind Randl to shield him from the wind. His voice was only a whisper, but it had a hard edge. The baby's thin, terrible wail was still in his ears.

"Is it true, Jakk? Do you know? Because if they are...."

Randl laughed and shuddered with a secret, ugly triumph. "I crawled up on the peak during the last darkness. The guards were cold and the wind made them blind and deaf. I lay in the rocks and watched. And I saw...."

He coughed. The Officers' voices rang sharp through the wind. Compact groups of men began to run, off toward the west. The whisper of sound had grown louder in Kirk's ears. He could hear men yelling and the ringing of metal on stone.

He started to run, holding Randl's elbow. Grey dust blew under their feet. The drifts of crystal stones sent their sound shivering back at them in

10

splinters. Kirk said fiercely:

"What did you see?"

They were passing under the hill now. Randl jerked his head. "Up there, Wes."

Kirk looked up. Someone was standing at the doorway of the Captain's hut. Someone tall and slender and the color of the Sunstar from head to foot.

"I saw her," said Randl hoarsely. "She was carrying heat-stones into the Ship."

Kirk's pupils shrank to points no warmer nor softer than the tip of his knife. He smiled, almost gently, looking up the hill.

The captain's yellow daughter, taking life into the Ship.

*

It was a big raid. Kirk saw that when he scrambled up out of the last gully, half-carrying the wheezing Randl. The Piruts had come up the tongue of rock between two deep cuts and tackled the guards' pillbox head on. They hadn't taken it, not yet. But they were still trying, piling up their dead on the swept grey stone.

They were using shags again. They drove the lumbering beasts on into the hail of stones and thrown spears from the pillbox, keeping low behind them, and then climbing on the round hairy bodies. It took courage, because sometimes the shags turned and clawed the men who drove them, and sometimes the dead ones weren't quite dead and it was too bad for the man who climbed on them.

It looked to Kirk as though the pillbox was pretty far gone.

He ran down the slope with the others, slipping in the crystal drifts. Randl was spent. Kirk kept him going, thinking of the huts back there on the plain, and Ma and Lil and the little ones, and the baby. You had to fight the Piruts, no matter what you thought about the Officers. You had to keep them from getting onto the plain.

He wondered about Pa. Hunting shags in the outer gullies was mean work any time, but when the Piruts were raiding....

THRALLS OF THE ENDLESS NIGHT

No time to think about that. Wite, the second son of the First Officer, was signalling for double time. Kirk ran faster, his ears twitching furiously as they sifted the flying echoes into some kind of order.

Pa hadn't been alone, of course. Frank and Russ went with him. The three of them would have sense enough to keep safe. Maybe they were in the pillbox.

A big raid. More Piruts than he'd ever seen before. He wondered why. He wondered how so many of them had been able to get so close to the pillbox all at once, walking two or three abreast on the narrow tongue of rock under the spears and slingstones.

They poured in through the gates of the stone-walled building, scattering up onto the parapet. There were slits in the rooms below and rusty metal things crouching behind them, but they weren't any good for fighting. A man needed shoulder room for spear and sling.

It was pretty hot up there. The wall of bodies had built up so high, mostly with shags, that the Piruts were coming right over the wall. Kirk's nose wrinkled at the smell of blood. He avoided the biggest puddles and found a place to stand between the dead.

Randl went down on his knees. He was coughing horribly, but his hot black eyes saw everything. He tried three times to lift his sling and gave it up.

"I'll cover you," said Kirk. He began taking crystal pebbles out of a big pile that was kept there and hurling them at the Piruts. They made a singing noise in the air, and they didn't stop going when they hit. They were heavy for their size, very heavy, with sharp edges.

Randl said, "Something funny, Wes. Too many Piruts. They couldn't risk 'em on an ordinary raid."

Kirk grunted. A Pirut with red hair standing straight in the wind came over the wall. Kirk speared him left-handed in the belly, dodged the downstroke of his loaded sap, and kicked the body out of the way.

He said, "Wonder how they got so close, so fast?"

"Some trick." Randl laughed suddenly. "Funny their wanting the Ship as much as you and I do."

"Think they could know what's in it?"

Randl's narrow shoulders twitched. "Near as we know, their legend is the same as ours. Something holy in the Ship, sacred and tabu. Only difference is they want to get it for themselves, and we want to keep it." He coughed and spat in sudden angry disgust. "And we've swallowed that stuff. We've let the Officers hoard heat and food so they can live no matter what happens to us. We're fools, Wes! A lot of bloody fools!"

He got up and began jabbing with his spear at heads that poked up over the wall.

*

The Piruts began to slack off. Stones still whistled past Kirk's head—a couple of them had grazed him by now—and spears showered down, but they weren't climbing the walls any more.

Randl grounded his spear, gasping. "That's that. Pretty soon they'll break, and then we can start thinking about...."

He stopped. Kirk put a stone accurately through the back of a Pirut's head and said grimly:

"Yeah. About what *we're* going to do."

Randl didn't answer. He sat down suddenly, doubled over. Kirk grinned. "Take it easy," he said softly. "I'll cover you."

Randl whispered, "Wes. Wes!" He held up one thin hand. Kirk let his own drop, looking at it. There was blood on it, running clear to the elbow.

He went down beside Randl, putting his arms around him, trying to see. Randl shook him off.

"Don't move me, you fool! Just listen." His voice was harsh and rapid. He was holding both hands over the left side of his neck, where it joined the shoulder. Kirk could see the bright blood beating up through his fingers.

He said, "Jakk, I'll get the sawbones...."

Hot black eyes turned to his. Burnt-out fires in a face with the young beard hardly full on its sharp jaw.

"Sit down, Wes, quick, and listen. Sawbones is no good—and why would I want to go on living anyway?"

He smiled. Kirk had never seen him smile like that, without bitterness or pain. He sat down, crouched on the body of a man who lived only two huts away from him. The blood made little red fountains between Randl's fingers.

"It's up to you, Wes. You're the only one that really knows about the Ship. You'll do better than I would, anyhow. You're a fighter. You carry it on, so the Hans can live. Promise."

Kirk nodded. He couldn't say anything. The heat was dying in Randl's eyes.

"Listen, Wes. I saw the secret way into Ship. Bend closer, and listen...."

Kirk bent. He didn't move for a long time. After a while Randl's voice stopped, and then the blood wasn't pumping any more, just oozing. Randl's hands slid away, so that Kirk could see the hole the stone had made. Everything seemed to be very quiet.

Kirk sat there, holding Randl in his arms.

Presently someone came up and shook Kirk's shoulder and said, "Hey, kid, are you deaf? We been yelling for you." He stopped, and then said more gently, "Oh. Jakk got it, did he?"

Kirk laid the body carefully on the stones and got up. "Yeah."

"Kind of a pal of yours, wasn't he?"

"He wasn't very strong. He needed someone to cover him."

"Too bad." The man shook his head, and then shrugged. "Maybe it's better, at that. He was headed for trouble, that one. Kinda leading you that way, too, I heard. Always talking."

He looked at Kirk's face and shut up suddenly. He turned away and grunted over his shoulders, "The O.D.'s looking for you."

Kirk followed. The wind was cold, howling up from the outer gullies.

*

The Officer of the Day was waiting at the north end of the wall. There was a ladder dropped over it now, and men were climbing up and down with bodies and sheaves of recovered spears. More were busy down below, rolling the dead Piruts and the shags down into the deep gullies for the scavenger rats and the living shags who didn't mind turning cannibal.

That ladder made Kirk think of Pa. It was the only way for a man to get

14

into the outer gullies from the west escarpment of the colony. He shook some of the queer heaviness out of his head, touched his forelock and said:

"I'm Wes Kirk, sir. You wanted me?"

"Yes." The O.D. was also the Third Officer. Taller than Kirk, thinner, with the hair going grey on his body and exhausted eyes sunk deep under his horny overlids. He said quietly:

"I'm sorry to have to tell you this...."

Kirk knew. The knowledge leaped through him. It was strange, to feel a spear-stab where there was no spear.

He said, "Pa."

The Officer nodded. He seemed very tired, and he didn't look at Kirk. He hadn't, after the first glance.

"Your father, and his two friends."

Kirk shivered. The horny lids dropped over his eyes. "I wish I'd known," he whispered. "I'd have killed more of them."

The Officer put his hands flat on the top of the wall and looked at them as if they were strange things and no part of him.

"Kirk," he said, "this is going to be hard to explain. I've never done anything as hard. The Piruts didn't kill them. They were responsible, but they didn't actually kill them."

Wes raised his head slowly. "I don't understand."

"We saw them coming up the tongue of rock. The Piruts were behind them, but not far. Not far enough. One of the three, it wasn't your father, called to us to put the ladder down. We waited...."

A muscle began to twitch under Kirk's eye. That, too, was something that had never happened before, like the stab of pain with no spear behind it. He licked his lips and repeated hoarsely:

"I don't understand."

The Officer tightened suddenly and made one hand into a fist and beat it slowly on the wall, up and down.

"I didn't want to give the order. God knows I didn't want to! But there was nothing else to do."

THRALLS OF THE ENDLESS NIGHT

A man came up over the top of the ladder. He was carrying a body over his shoulder, and breathing hard.

"Here's Kirk," he said. "Where'll I put him?"

There was a clear space off to the right. Kirk pointed to it. "Over there, Charley. I'll help."

It was hard to move. He'd never been tired like this before. He'd never been afraid like this, either. He didn't know what he was afraid of. Something in the Officer's voice.

He helped to lay his father down. He'd seen bodies before. He'd handled them, fighting on the pillbox walls. But never one he'd known so long, one he'd eaten and slept and wrestled with. The thick arm that hauled him out of bed this morning, the big hands that warmed the baby against the barrel chest. You saw it lying lax and cold, but you didn't believe it.

You saw it. You saw the spear shaft sticking out clean from the heart....

You saw it....

"That's one of our spears!" He screamed it, like a woman. "One of our own—from the front!"

"I let them get as close as I dared," said the Officer tonelessly. "I tried to find a way. But there wasn't any way but the ladder, and that was what the Piruts wanted. That's why they made them come."

Kirk's voice wasn't a voice at all. "You killed them. You killed my father."

"Three lives, against all those back on the plain. We held our fire too long as it was, hoping. The Piruts nearly broke through. Try to understand! I had to do it."

Kirk's spear made a flat clatter on the stone. He started forward. Men moved in and held him, without rancor, looking at their own feet.

"Please try to understand," whispered the Officer. "I had to do it."

The Officer, the bloody wall, the stars and the cold grey gullies all went away. There was nothing but darkness, and wind, a long way off. Kirk thought of Pa coming up under the wall, close to safety, close enough to touch it, and no way through. Pa and Frank and Russ, standing under the wall, looking up, and no way through.

16

Looking up, calling to the men they knew, asking for help and getting a spear through the heart.

After that, even the wind was gone, and the darkness had turned red.

*

There was a voice, a long way off. It said, "God, he's strong!" Over and over. It got louder. There were weights on his arms and legs, and he couldn't throw them off. He was pressed against something.

It was the wall. He saw that after a while. The wall where the Officer had been standing. There were six men holding him, three on each side. The Officer was gone.

Kirk relaxed. He was shivering and covered with rime from body sweat. Somebody whistled.

"Six men! Didn't know the kid had it in him."

The Officer's voice said dully, "No discipline. Better take him home."

Kirk tried to turn. The six men swung with him. Kirk said, "You better discipline me. You better kill me, because, if you don't, I'll kill you."

"I don't blame you, boy. Go and rest. You'll understand."

"I'll understand, all right." Kirk's voice was a hoarse, harsh whisper that came out by itself and wouldn't be stopped. "I'll understand about Pa, and the Ship with the heat-stones in it, and the Captain's yellow daughter getting fat and warm while my sisters freeze and go hungry. I'll understand, and I'll make everybody else understand, too!"

The Officer's eyes held a quick fire. "Boy! Do you know what you're saying?"

"You bet I know!"

"That's mutiny. For God's sake, don't make things worse!"

"Worse for us, or for you?" Kirk was shouting, holding his head up in the wind. "Listen, you men! Do you know what the Officers are doing up there in the Ship they won't let us touch?"

There was an uneasy stirring among the Hans, a slipping aside of luminous black eyes. The Officer shut his jaw tight. He stepped in close to Kirk.

"Shut up," he said urgently. "Don't make me punish you, not now. You're talking rot, but it's dangerous."

Kirk's eyes were hot and not quite sane. He couldn't have stopped if he'd wanted to.

"Rot, is it? Jakk Randl knew. He saw with his own eyes and he told me while he was dying. The Captain's yellow daughter, sneaking heat-stones into...."

The Officer hit him on the jaw, carefully and without heat. Kirk sagged down. The Officer stepped back, looking as though he had a pain in him that he didn't want to show.

He said quietly, but so that everyone could hear him, "Discipline, for not longer than it takes to clear the rock below."

Two of the men nodded and took Kirk away down a flight of stone steps. One of the four who were left looked over the wall and spat.

"Rock's pretty near clean," he said, "but even so...." He shook himself like a dog. "That Jakk Randl, he was always talking."

One of the others flicked a quick look around and whispered, "Yeah. And maybe he knew what he was talking about!"

*

The little stone room was cold and quiet. It was dark, too, but the sucking-plant carried its own light. Kirk lay on his back watching the cool green fire pulse on his chest and belly. It looked cool, but underneath the sprawling tentacles of it he was burning with the pain of little needles that bit and sucked.

He was spreadeagled with leather thongs. He made no sound. The sweat ran into his eyes and the blood went out of his body into the hungry plant, drop by drop.

Somebody came in, somebody too quick and light to be a fighting man. Kirk let his pupils spread. First a slim tall shape moving, a kilt of little skins swirling beneath the shimmering sinthi-mesh overall suit. Small sharp breasts and a heavy mane of hair caught back.

Then color. Yellow. Yellow like the Sunstar, from head to foot. Kirk's jaw shut and knotted.

The sucking-plant was ripped away very deftly by its upper fronds and thrown into a corner. Kirk went rigid, but he didn't make a sound. The yellow girl took a knife from her belt sheath and slashed him free with four quick strokes.

Kirk didn't move.

"Well," she said. "Aren't you going to get up?"

He could see her eyes, great black shining things. "What did you come here for?"

"They told me about you. I said I thought it was criminal to discipline you when you didn't know what you were doing. So I came down to see what I could do about it."

She always came with the other women after a raid, to help the wounded. Kirk looked at her stonily.

"You must have just missed my speech."

"They told me about it. Whatever made you say things like that?"

"Aren't they true?"

"No!"

Kirk laughed. It was not a pleasant laugh. "You could have saved yourself the trouble. This isn't going to make me believe you."

The girl tossed her thick hair back impatiently. "You're acting like a child." She was no older than Kirk. "We're all terribly sorry about your father," she went on gravely, "but that doesn't give you the right...."

"I have the right to tell the truth."

"But you're not telling the truth!" She was down on her knees now, beside him. "I don't know what this Jakk Randl saw, or whether he saw anything, but...."

Kirk said slowly, "Jakk's dead. He was my friend, and he didn't lie."

"Perhaps not. But he was mistaken."

"He saw you, taking heat-stones into the Ship."

"But only a very few! We're not hoarding them. We wouldn't!"

"Then what do you use them for?"

"I can't tell you that. And it doesn't matter anyway."

THRALLS OF THE ENDLESS NIGHT

Kirk laughed again. He got up, stiffly because of the raw places drawing across the front of him. His hair was gone in a sprawling pattern, eaten off by digestive acids. He said:

"You'll have to do better than that."

She was angry, now, and perhaps a little scared. He enjoyed making her angry and scared. He enjoyed the thick hot feeling of power it gave him.

She asked, "Then you won't believe, and you won't stop talking?"

"I made a promise to go on talking. And I believe in what I'm doing."

"You know what that will mean." He could hear the quiver and the breathing of her. "People may be hurt, your own people. We don't want trouble. We can't afford trouble, with the Piruts getting stronger. It'll mean you'll be punished, maybe even—killed."

That gave him a cold twinge for a moment. Then he thought of Jakk and shrugged.

"It doesn't matter," he said, and started out.

The Third Officer came in. There were five men with him, and one of them was the Captain, wearing the gun of authority.

The Captain said, "I'm sorry, Kirk. I heard a lot of what you said; too much to dare turn you loose just now. Perhaps in solitary we can talk sense into you."

Kirk stood quite still, not moving anything but his eyes. The four Hans were big and they had knives. Kirk shrugged and fell in with them. The girl walked ahead, between the Captain and the Third.

Nobody said anything. They went together up the stone steps.

*

They had taken the wounded off the wall, out of the wind. The rock below was clean of bodies, and the last of the men were coming back up the ladder.

Kirk felt queer. He wasn't like himself at all. It was as though he had fragments of ice inside his head, all jumbled. Then suddenly they fell into place, clear and frozen and unalterable, without any help from him at all.

He moved, very fast. Faster than ever before in his life, caught the Captain's gun.

20

His two hands thrust out, one against the Captain, the other against the Third, and sent them staggering. He charged through between them, gathering the yellow girl in to his chest firing as he went. The antique gun went dead on the third shot, and he threw it away.

A knife slashed across his shoulders, but it was short. Men began to yell. He knocked one away from the ladder head and pushed the struggling girl over and let her drop, so that she had to catch the rungs. He whirled, swinging, and sent two men sprawling back into the ones behind. Then he leaped over, dropping down the side of the ladder hand over hand.

He passed the girl, climbed onto the ladder behind her so that no one could sling stones at him, and began pulling her down by the foot. She tried kicking, but it was a long drop to the rock, and after she'd slipped a couple of times she stopped that and went on down.

Men were howling at him from above. They started to climb onto the ladder. Kirk yelled at them, threatening to throw the girl off. They stopped. Presently Kirk felt the cold rock underfoot.

The minute he was off the ladder a man climbed over the wall and started down. Kirk yelled at him to go back, then got hold of the bottom of the ladder and pushed out. The yellow girl got out her knife again and slashed at him. She hadn't opened her mouth once.

Kirk dropped. The knife bit his shoulder, not very deep. He straightened up suddenly, swinging his open palm. It caught the girl over the ear. She fell backward away from him, rolling over on the rock. The knife flew out of her hand. Kirk heard it skitter along and then vanish over the gully edge.

He pushed hard on the ladder. It gave, and the man at the top began scrambling up again, fast. He only just made it, dangling half of him in the air, when the ladder fell. The light aluminum struts it was made of sent clashing echoes flying in the wind.

It was the only ladder they had. They'd have to bring one from one of the other pillboxes before they could climb down and get it. Kirk looked up at the men lining the wall, yelling, waving things.

Just about here Pa must have stood, looking up.

THRALLS OF THE ENDLESS NIGHT

He turned and hauled the dazed girl to her feet and started off down the tongue of rock. He didn't hurry. There was no need to hurry. The young strength of the girl was pressed against him, thigh and hip and chest. It burned, in some queer way.

He watched the yellow hairs rub and tangle with his golden ones. The muscle started twitching under his eye again.

He had to cuff her twice more to keep her quiet, before they were safely off the naked rock. He got her down the length of two gullies, well out of sight of the pillbox. She was still a little groggy, and very busy keeping her footing in the pebble drifts. They started down a third cut that angled off. Then, quite suddenly, she fell.

Kirk stopped. He put out a hand to help her up, and then took it back again. He looked at his feet and surlily, "Get up."

"I can't. Where are you going?"

"I don't know. Just somewhere to think, and plan. I've got to figure this out."

She thought about that. He could see her wide golden shoulders tremble. He wanted to touch them. After a while she said:

"Why did you take me? Why won't you let me go?"

"They'd have killed me on the rock if I hadn't had you. And when I go back...."

She brought her head up. "You're going *back?*"

He laughed at her. "Did you think you could get rid of me that easy? I told you I'd made a promise. I'm going to keep it, and you're going to help me. I can buy a lot with you."

Her pupils were little hot pinpoints. "I see. You don't care how many people you hurt, do you, as long as you can be a big man and keep your promise."

He said roughly, "Get up."

"All right." She nodded, casually. "I'll get up."

She did. She got up fast, like a rocksnake uncoiling, and she had a big stone in her right hand. She let it go, straight for his head.

Kirk jerked himself aside, but he was too late. The rock grazed him above the ear. He staggered, trying to see through a curtain of hot and flashing lights.

His earcups, working instinctively by themselves, brought him the sound of naked feet scrambling away over the pebble drifts.

Feet. And then something else....

Kirk yelled. He tried to shake the lights away, and yelled again.

"Stop! Look out—*shags!*"

*

He heard her stop. He began to be able to see again. She was poised halfway up the head wall of the cut, her ears twitching. For a long time they stood that way, not moving, listening to the wind and the rolling pebbles and the soft padding feet of things that were hungry and hunting them.

She began to move, almost without sound, back to him. Her lips formed the word "Two," and her yellow head jerked back the way she had been going. Kirk nodded. He pointed off to the left and held up three fingers. Then he turned and started down the gully. The girl stayed close beside him. She was breathing rapidly and her pupils swelled and shrank. They showed no fear.

Looking at them, Kirk thought of Lil. Lil was right. She did have pink lids to her eyes, and they were beautiful.

The shags followed them, two behind, three beside them beyond a thin wall of rock.

Kirk had never been in the outer gullies before. He was too young. But he'd heard Pa and the older men talk about them from the time he was old enough to crouch beside the heat-stones and listen.

Out here there were shags and scavenger rats and once in a while a rocksnake. Men of the settlement never hunted beyond the fringe. Beyond that was forbidden ground and Piruts. Nobody knew just where the Pirut colony was any more. Nobody wanted to know.

Kirk's ears were stretched, sifting the tiny shattered echoes. His spread pupils sucked in every bit of the dim grey light. His body hair was erect so that even his skin acted as a sensory organ, feeling the bodies of the shags behind them.

They were getting close.

The gully ended. Beyond it was a little space of tumbled rock with other gullies opening into it, and then a cliff built of great tilted slabs of grey stone.

Kirk pointed to the cliff and started to run, with the yellow girl beside him. Wind slashed sharp and thin across them. The echoes whispered like many tongues and Kirk fought them and heard the two shags come onto the plain behind them, running.

The other three came out of the parallel cut. They came fast, and because of the curve of the plain they were a little ahead of the two humans.

The girl said between her teeth, "We can't make it."

She was right. Kirk picked out the biggest boulder he could see and dashed for it. The leading shag was breathing on the girl's heels as he hauled her up after him.

They were safe for a while, but it didn't do them any good. In this world even shags would wait forever at the prospect of a square meal. Presently they'd start climbing and when they did it was all over. Kirk didn't even have a weapon with which to fight.

He looked down at them. Five squat thick shapes with six legs; four powerful legs with claws and two slender ones held in against the chest, armed with sucker discs for climbing. Five pairs of black eyes watching, hungry and infinitely patient. Five tucked bellies burning under pale, shaggy hair.

He was looking at death. A strange cold terror took him. He turned his head toward the yellow girl and saw the same thing in her eyes. They looked at each other, not moving nor breathing, thinking that they were young and going to die.

He shivered. The girl's yellow body burned in the grey light. He moved. He didn't know why, only that he had to. He took her in his arms and found her lips and kissed them, roughly, with an urgent, painful hunger. She fought him a little and then lay still against him.

One of the shags started to climb. Kirk saw it across the girl's shoulder. He let her go and walked to the boulder's edge and waited until the shaggy head was level with his feet. Then he crouched and struck, in a way he had never struck before. Blood spurted across his fist. The shag roared and fell backward clumsily, shaking its head. Kirk stood up and sucked in his belly and yelled. He felt savage now, but not afraid. The echoes howled eerily.

The shag started up again, and two more came with him.

There was something queer about the echoes. They got louder and wilder. Men's voices, shouting. Kirk couldn't look, but he heard the yellow girl cry: "Piruts!"

*

He heard them coming closer, bare feet scrambling on rock. The shags came higher. He struck down, left and right. One beast lost hold with one sucker and fell into another, knocking it loose. They fell, clawing each other. The third came on. Kirk hit it. It slid its head aside and caught his wrist.

The pain blinded him. He roared and beat at it, but the grip on his wrist pulled him to his knees and almost over the edge. The brute started back down the boulder, taking Kirk with him.

The yellow girl slid suddenly in under Kirk and reached over and took hold of the shag's snout and peeled it back. The beast snuffled and squealed and chewed on Kirk's arm. The girl twisted harder. Blood began to spill down over the shag's teeth.

It let go. Kirk began to hear slingstones whistle. The shag bellowed and took itself back down the rock, fast. The others were scattering away across the plain, driven by stones from expert slingers. Kirk and the girl crouched quietly, trembling and breathing hard.

Somebody called cheerfully, "You might as well come down now."

Kirk supposed they might as well. He climbed down, streaming blood from his torn wrist, with the girl scrambling beside him. The hackles were raised across her yellow shoulders.

Piruts. Kirk thought about Pa and Russ and Frank being driven up that tongue of naked rock. Their own people had killed them, but the Piruts put them there in the first place. And there was Jakk. Besides....

They were Piruts. That was enough. Kirk felt numb inside. It might have been easier if the shags had got them, after all.

The man who had called them was waiting, lounging back against a rock. He was no taller than Kirk, but he was a lot thicker and his hair was red. The bones of his face were heavy and brutal under his beard. His horny overlids were dropped so that only bright black slits showed of his eyes. He was smiling. It was a lazy, white-toothed, cheerful smile, but Kirk didn't like. It made his belly knot up.

"What," said the Pirut, "the hell are you two kids doing out here?"

"Hunting," said Kirk shortly. There were a lot of Piruts among the tumbled rocks. Four, five hands of them.

The red Pirut had stopped looking at Kirk. He was looking at the Captain's yellow daughter. "Well," he said. "Well, well!" He took himself away from the rock and came toward them. He moved slowly, as though he might be sleepy. Kirk didn't like that, either.

He said, "Let us go. We haven't anything to steal."

The Pirut chuckled. "I'm not so sure about that." He was still looking at the yellow girl. "No," he said. "I'm not sure about that at all."

He raised his hand and called the others in. Kirk knew he couldn't fight; he followed the leader.

*

It was a lot colder in the Pirut cave than it was back in the huts of the colony. Everybody kept close together for warmth, crowded around the scanty heat-stones. There was a moaning draft from somewhere that kept Kirk's hair stirring, and there were babies crying. Babies that didn't sound any different from the one at home.

Kirk chewed up the last of his handful of pemmican, made of shag meat and sour berries, and was thankful for a full belly. The yellow girl crouched on the cold stone, not saying anything, her arms around her knees. The Pirut women watched her out of hostile eyes.

Samel, the red Pirut who had turned out to be some sort of an Officer, watched her too, but his eyes were not hostile.

"Close-mouthed piece, aren't you?" he said. He threw a scrap of bone at a wiry black girl huddled over the heat, and laughed. "Sada," he yelled, "get her to give you lessons, will you?"

Everybody enjoyed that. Sada called him a name and turned her back. Samel's black eyes came back to the yellow girl.

"You won't tell who you are. That means you're somebody. An Officer's daughter, likely. Maybe even the Captain's."

Some flicker in the girl's eyes must have told him he'd hit home. He jumped up and shouted, "Hey! All of you, look here! We've got somebody—we've got the Captain's daughter!"

The mob stirred and moved in. People began to shout, to curse and make animal noises of sheer hate. For a minute Kirk thought he and the girl were going to be torn apart. He shivered violently, and the hate was so strong in the air he could smell it.

Samel pulled out his sling lazily and loaded it. The sweep of his arm stopped part of the crowd, and the rest quieted down enough to hear him say:

"Hold it! Sit down, you fools! The girl's gold. We can buy things with her."

Kirk didn't get that word 'gold', but he understood the rest of it. It was what he had told her, himself.

He wished the babies would stop crying. It was hard to hate these people so much when you knew they had kids just like the one at home, wailing in the cold.

The mob relaxed sullenly. The Captain's daughter spoke suddenly, very clear across the muttering quiet of the crowd.

"You can't buy your way into the colony with me. They'll kill me, like they did the three Hans, only this time they won't wait as long."

She was telling the truth. Samel didn't like it, and Kirk liked it even less, but she was. The muscle twitched under Kirk's eye. It was a hell of a world. You couldn't keep straight in it at all.

THRALLS OF THE ENDLESS NIGHT

"All right," said Samel. "But we can buy heat with you. And maybe before we do we can get some things out of you, *free*." He moved in close to her, staring down with sultry eyes. He said huskily, "And don't think we can't, baby. And don't think we wouldn't enjoy it!"

She shivered, but her eyes didn't flinch. She told him steadily, "If it's about the Ship, you can do what you want and go to hell with it."

"I watched you up there on that rock," said Samel slowly. "Both of you. You have guts, all right. But I wonder...." He let his gaze slide down over her long, arrogant body. "It would be a pity to spoil that."

*

The girl Sada pushed her way out from the crowd.

"You big red son of a she-shag! Look at us! Look at this lousy cave, and those boxes of heat-stones that wouldn't keep a rat-pup warm, and then think of these swine sitting up there on their plateau, fat and happy, toasting their feet! *They* drove us out here to starve and freeze. *They're* robbing the gullies of heat-stones. Listen to those kids crying! They haven't been warm since they were born, and whose fault is it? And you worry about spoiling that yellow vixen!"

Samel said pleasantly, "Shut up that screeching." He shoved the girl aside hard enough to sit her down on the stones and then knelt beside the Captain's daughter. He pulled her head back by the yellow hair and looked down into her eyes and said:

"But she's right. Pretty soon there aren't going to be any more heat-stones at all. Pretty soon we're all going to die of the cold. But you won't, you up there on the plateau. You can watch us freeze on the rocks and feel pretty smart about it. And you'll have the Ship."

He drew his breath in, sharp, as though something hurt him. His horny lids dropped and his lips twisted like a child about to cry with pain. His hand tightened suddenly in the girl's hair, jerking her head back hard on the taut curve of her neck. He slapped her twice across the face and let her go and stood up, backing off and trembling.

"You'll have the Ship," he whispered, "for always."

Kirk got up. He felt sick, and there were red clouds across his eyes. The Captain's yellow daughter. He'd cuffed her himself. Why did this happen to him when somebody else did it? It was a hell of a world and he was lost in it. All he knew was that he wanted to hit Samel hard enough to kill him.

Instead somebody hit Kirk from behind with a sap, not very hard. He fell on his face. From a great distance he heard the girl Sada screaming:

"You and your silly Ship! What does the Ship matter when we're all going to die?"

"It matters." Samel's voice was husky and queer. "It's the beginning and the end. What it has in it belongs to us. It would make us fat and warm and strong, so that we could rule the whole world. My father died trying to reach it, and his father before him, and *his* father before that. The Ship matters. It's everything."

It was still in the cave. It was as though his voice had wiped it clean of sound. Kirk shivered. And in the silence the babies cried, a thin wailing lamentation to the cold.

Kirk got up on his knees. "Wait a minute," he said thickly. "Wait, you're going at this wrong. We all are. Wait, and listen to me."

*

Samel looked at him as though he'd forgotten Kirk existed. Somebody said, "Shall I fix him, Boss?" Samel started to nod, and then something in Kirk's face changed his mind.

"He put up a good fight out there. Let him talk."

Kirk got his feet under him. His head throbbed, and falling on his bandaged wrist hadn't done it any good, but at least he could see, and talk. He was scared, because what he was going to say was against everything he'd been taught since he was born, but he had to say it. There might be a lot of things wrong with it, but basically it was right, and he knew it. He knew Jakk Randl would have said it, too.

He did not look at the Captain's yellow daughter.

"Listen," he said, loud enough so that everyone could hear him. "You're wrong about one thing. We don't have heat-stones up there on the plateau.

THRALLS OF THE ENDLESS NIGHT

Not the people like me, the little guys, the Hans. We starve and freeze just like you do, and our babies cry just as loud. And we sit, like you do, looking at the Ship and wondering."

He took a deep breath. They were watching him, not believing nor disbelieving. Just listening, feeling him, waiting for something he said to hit them so they'd know whether he was lying or not.

"Some of us have wondered a lot lately, about that Ship. The Officers don't let us near it. They never have, no nearer than you out here in the gullies. But somebody *did* get close to it, one man who believed in what he was doing, and he saw...."

He told them what Jakk had seen, thinking about Jakk's blood running red through his fingers and the fire dying in his eyes.

"I'm a Ship's man. I've been taught to hate and fear you. You killed my friend. But the Officers killed my father, without even trying to save him. And I think we're fools, we Hans and you Piruts. We're all just people, with empty stomachs and cold backs and kids that never get warm. Why should we kill each other at those walls?"

He had them. He could hear the mob suck its breath in like one man. Samel's eyes were hot enough to burn. Kirk cried out:

"It's the Officers we ought to hate! It's the Officers who hold the Ship, and hide the heat-stones in it! It's the Officers we ought to fight, not each other!"

The mob screamed out of a single throat. Out of the tail of his eye Kirk saw the yellow girl spring up. Her hands were clenched and her face was a mask of horror, of hatred and a strange pleading. She was saying something, but the mob yell drowned her words, and when it died down somebody had the girl, holding her arms and her mouth.

"All right," said Samel hoarsely, and licked his lips. "All right. What are you going to do about it? What's your scheme?"

"I'm going to take you there, the secret way. I'm going to take you to the Ship, so that we can break the Officers and live, together."

He did not look at the Captain's yellow daughter.

*

LEIGH BRACKETT

The northern escarpment of the plateau fell sheer into a deep gorge. Kirk led them into it, Samel and six hands of Pirut men and the yellow girl with a strip of hide to gag her mouth. The darkness had come down, so thick and black that pupils at their widest spread could hardly make anything from the starshine. They went slowly, but almost without sound.

Kirk watched the dead Ship, thrusting high above them against the cold stars. Presently he stopped and whispered, "Here, I think."

They stopped. Kirk went alone to the cliff wall and felt along it. His hands slipped behind a curtain of moss, into a crack barely big enough for a man's shoulder. There seemed to be a blank wall beyond, but he felt sideways, and found that Jakk had been right. There was a way.

He went back to Samel. "It's there. Come on."

"No!" Samel caught his arm. He was looking up, at the broken Ship on the cliff-top, and he was trembling. "Wait," he whispered. "I want to know this, to keep it."

Kirk followed his rapt stare. The Ship, brooding over the plain, dominant even in death. The Ship that had brought them, Officers and Hans, in some strange forgotten way from some forgotten place, and died in the bringing. The Ship, Untouchable....

Kirk shivered, violently. His heartbeats choked him. And then Samel was speaking, no louder than a whisper, to the night and the Ship.

"We came from the sky, following, hunting. It had power and gold in its belly, and they kept us from it. They kept us Outside, away from the Ship, and we starved and froze and waited. And now we're going in." He caught his breath between his teeth and shuddered. "And now we're going in!"

Kirk whispered, "What are 'power' and 'gold'?"

"I don't know. Something in the legend. Something men live for, and die for. We'll know soon."

"We'll know soon. Samel, remember the bargain. No killing or plundering among the Hans."

Samel smiled, but the muscles ran hard along his jaw.

THRALLS OF THE ENDLESS NIGHT

"If you're telling the truth, there won't be any reason for it. We'll let the Officers decide whether *they* die or not." Samel started forward. "The Ship," he said softly, and laughed. "*The Ship!*"

They went toward the cleft in the rock. Somebody said, "Hey, it's warm in this gorge!" Kirk realized then that he wasn't cold, and wondered why. Then he smiled bitterly. Sure. The Officers had found a vein of heat-stones, probably just under the soil where they were standing. The gorge had never been a source of the stones, the crystal rocks that looked just like the ones scattered all over except that they had a tiny light in them and burned you when you picked them up. But the Officers must be getting them from here and taking them up to the Ship, to hoard.

Most of his superstitious chill went away when he thought about that.

Inside the cleft was a shaft leading up, tool-shaped here and there, with rusty metal bars set in the rock. Kirk led the way. There was no sound made loud enough to be heard over the wind that blew across the plateau. Kirk and Samel came up out of the shaft and took the two guards from behind easily enough, and went on to the Ship.

Just for a moment, looking down across the plain, thinking about Ma Kirk and Lil and the little ones, Kirk was scared. He'd let the Piruts in. If Samel didn't keep his word, if anything....

But nothing would go wrong. There was no reason for it to. He was telling the truth, and once the Ship was broken into there was no quarrel between the Piruts and the Hans. They were allies against the Officers.

He remembered what he'd said to Lil, about the Captain's yellow daughter.

Samel left a guard behind and went into the Ship.

Darkness and cold and the smell of a place that hasn't been used or lived in for a long, long time, and the grit of rusty metal under bare feet. They went very slowly, and the yellow girl whimpered in her gag.

They couldn't really be silent, slipping and blundering in blackness too thick even for their eyes, over buckled deck plates and around broken walls. Somebody heard them and called out, and the yellow girl struggled like a speared shag.

Kirk shivered and the palms of his hands were wet. He could feel the Ship like a living presence in the dark.

The somebody called again, with fear in his voice. They stumbled down a long, tilted passageway and came into a little room with a great gash in it looking out over the gorge. There was a barred door in one wall, and a man sitting in front of it over a tiny box of heat-stones.

The Captain.

He got up, a lean grey man moving with dignity. He didn't drop his spear, but he didn't try to use it, either. He didn't say anything. His eyes took them in, in the dull glow of the heat-stones—Kirk and Samel and the Piruts, and then the yellow girl, gagged and held by the arms. His eyes blazed, then. Kirk's heart jolted. It was just the way Pa might have looked at Lil.

He said roughly, thinking of Pa, "Don't try anything, and you won't get hurt. I've made a pact with the Piruts. There's to be no more fighting and we take the Ship together, share and share alike. The Officers can obey, or take what's coming to them. Where are the heat-stones?"

The Captain stared at him. His face had no expression. He said, "Let my daughter go."

Samel started forward. The Captain raised his spear. "Let my daughter go!" The Piruts raised their weapons. Samel looked around the room, at the single door behind them, and grinned.

"Sure," he said. "Why not? Let her go."

They let her go. She tore off the gag and ran to her father and stood by him, glaring at the Piruts with hot black eyes. Neither one said anything.

"All right," said Samel lazily. "Now where are the stones?"

"There." The Captain pointed at the tiny box at his feet. "Those are all the heat-stones there are in the Ship."

Kirk cried, "That's a lie!"

The Captain looked at him. "Tell your friends to go and search."

"What about that door behind you?"

"There are no stones in there."

Kirk laughed. The laugh was not pleasant. He was thinking of the cold huts of the Hans and the thin babies that cried, and Jakk Randl dying on the pillbox wall, telling him what he'd seen.

"You lie. You bring the stones up out of the gorge and hide them here. Jakk Randl saw your daughter doing it."

"There was only a tiny pipe of stones in the gorge. This is almost the last of them. We used them rather than take from the community supply."

Samel smiled his lazy smile and started toward the barred door. His eyes had a queer wild shine to them. The Captain cried out:

"Wait! Wait, and let me speak!"

Samel looked at the door and his breath made a little sob in his throat. "All right," he said hoarsely. "I can wait."

He wasn't thinking about the heat-stones so much then. He was thinking of the words of the legend, power and gold.

The Captain said quietly, "You can kill me, and go on. But I ask you not to. I ask you to believe me. There are no heat-stones in that room. The bar hasn't been lifted since the Crash. I ask you not to violate a sacred trust."

Kirk scowled and looked at the bar. It didn't look as though it had been lifted since the Crash. He began to be uneasy.

Samel spoke silkily. "Sacred trust, eh? Something that belongs to us, the Piruts. Something we've waited for, longer than anyone knows."

The Captain nodded. He seemed very tired. "I should have remembered that. The Legend grows a little hazy.... You Piruts caused the Crash. You followed our Ship and attacked it, and in the battle your own ship was destroyed. You made land somehow in little ships carried inside the big one. After we crashed you tried again to take what is in the Ship, and we drove you out into the gullies and kept you there."

"Ever since," answered Samel huskily. "Starving and freezing."

"We've starved and frozen, too, all of us—Officers and Hans alike. But we had a sacred trust in this Ship. We've guarded it. I think at first the Officers of that day thought that someone would come from—from wherever the Ship came from, and take them back. No one ever did. And in the struggle to live, everything has been lost. The only thing left is the knowledge that we Officers had a duty, a trust, and we've guarded this door night and day since the Crash."

"What's behind it?" asked Samel. "What's behind it?"

"Even that is lost."

Samel laughed and started forward. He caught the Captain's half-raised spear in his hands and broke it and pushed him away with the yellow girl. He took hold of the bar and lifted. Kirk and the packed mass of Piruts swayed forward like one man.

It fought him. He heaved on the bar, and sweat ran dark on his red body-hair and the veins stood like ropes on his forehead, but the rust held. Samel struggled, crying like a child.

Kirk thought: "He told the truth, the Captain did. No heat-stones, and I've let the Piruts in." He began to shiver. He started to shout—

The bar screamed like a man in torment and swung back in Samel's hands, and the door was open.

*

The pale glow of the heat-stones filtered through the opening. Kirk saw a box with black marks on it—DANGER. ATOBLAST HIGH EXPLOSIVE—and above that a much smaller box made of metal, on a shelf. The black marks on the first box didn't mean anything to anybody. The father of the Captain's great-grandfather had remembered that there was such a thing as reading.

Samel reached out and took the smaller box, which was at eye level, and locked with a heavy lock, and sealed. He put it down and took the Captain's broken spear and tore the lock away.

The Captain and his yellow daughter stood like dead things, watching. Kirk's heart was pounding in his throat. The secret of the Ship, the sacred thing, the gold and power that had caused the Crash—

Samel's big red hand pulled out a flat bundle of metal sheets, marked with marks like the first box.

Treaty of Alliance between the Sovereign Earth and the Union of Jovian Moons, providing for Earthly colonization and development of the said Moons, and mutual aid against Aggressor Worlds.

A single sheet fell out of the bundle. "*... have taken the precaution of sending the treaty secretly in a ship of colonists, in care of the captain who knows nothing of its nature. It has been rumored that our mutual enemy, the Martio-Venusian Alliance, may try to intercept it, possibly with the aid of hired pirates. This would, as you know, mean war. It is my prayer that the treaty will safely....*"

Samel stared at the bundle. He shook it, his face looking dazed, like a man just hit in the stomach. Then he threw it down and shook the box. It was empty. In a black fury he turned on the larger box and ripped the cover back, and there was nothing under it but thick transparent bottles with heavy caps, holding a tiny bit of matter in oily liquid.

There was silence in the room, thick with the breathing of stunned and angry men.

"Power," said Samel. "Power, and gold! Nothing! Nothing to make even a spear-head!"

He picked up the empty box and the bundle and hurled them out through the riven wall into the gorge. Then he caught up the larger box and threw it after.

Kirk had time to see tears running out of Samel's eyes. After that there was an agony of light and sound and motion, and then nothing.

The first thing he knew about was heat. More heat than he'd ever felt in his life, pouring over him. He opened his eyes.

Men were piled against the walls, beginning to struggle back to life. The Ship had changed position. Samel was crouched with his arms around his knees, motionless, staring at nothing. The yellow girl was helping her father out of a mound of Piruts. And it was hot.

There was light beating in through the broken wall. Kirk crawled over and peered out, his pupils contracted to little points.

The bottom of the gorge was split open, and it was burning. The father of the Captain's great-grandfather had remembered vaguely something about radioactivity and crystalline rocks that harnessed it and made heat. The father

36

of *his* great-grandfather had had great hopes for the unique form of radiation and what it could be made to do. But all his time was taken hunting meat and heat-stones, and growing moss.

The heavy heart of the little world was burning up through the crack, and for the first time, Kirk was really warm.

Kirk put his hand on Samel's shoulder. "You got heat," he said. "That's better than power and gold, whatever they are."

Samel shivered and closed his eyes. His hands went with blind speed to Kirk's throat and closed, hard. His mouth was twisted, like a child crying with pain.

*

Kirk clawed at his thumbs. "Don't be a fool!" he croaked. "There's heat now. Heat for everybody. The kids won't cry any more. Samel, bring your people in out of the gullies!"

"Heat," repeated Samel. "Yeah." He took his hands away slowly. "There's that, isn't there? Heat."

The Captain echoed, "Heat." He went to the broken wall and blinked at the light. "The heat-stones were almost gone. I thought we were going to die. And now...." He shook his shoulders, like a man freed of a burden. "Now there's no more need to guard the Ship. Perhaps that's what we've been guarding it for, to save us in time of need."

Kirk said humbly, "I'm sorry."

"You were honest. You believed you were right. But taking my daughter...."

"I deserve the sucking-plant."

"What's done is done, and it's turned out right."

People were clamoring outside the Ship. Kirk was sweating. He tasted it, and laughed, pulling in his belly and spreading his chest.

"Heat," he said. "And no more fighting with the Piruts. Maybe there's some way we can roof the gorge and bring the heat up into the fields so the moss will grow better. And there's a lot of this world out beyond the gullies. We've never been able to explore it because of the Piruts. Samel, do you know what lies beyond you?"

Samel shook his head. "We had to eat and hunt for heat-stones, too."

"A whole world," said Kirk, "just waiting for us. Maybe we'll find other gorges like this one. Maybe places with better soil. The kids can grow up warm and fat, and have kids of their own...."

He turned around and looked at the Captain's yellow daughter.

He said, "Do you still hate me?"

Her yellow shoulders twitched. She turned her back on him, and she was so beautiful he hurt with it. He went up behind her.

"I said I was sorry."

She didn't answer. A close-mouthed piece.

"I lied."

Her head jerked a little and her earcups moved.

"I'm not sorry I took you with me. I'm not sorry I kissed you on the rock. Are you sorry you saved my life?"

She tossed her head. "I didn't."

"You did so. You twisted that shag's nose half off. Why?"

She turned around, hot-eyed, and slapped him. He laughed. He took her in his arms and waited till she quit clawing and struggling. Then he kissed her. Presently she kissed him back.

"You don't talk much," he said. "But who wants talk?"

www.ingramcontent.com/pod-product-compliance
Lightning Source LLC
Chambersburg PA
CBHW021005150626
46549CB00012BA/1343